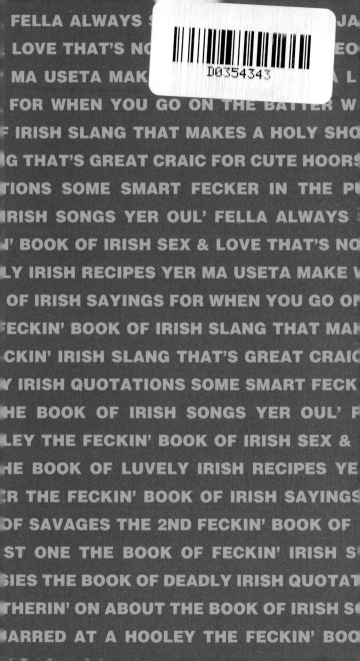

The 2nd
feckin' book of
Irish Slang
that makes a holy
show of the first one

The Feckin' Collection

The 2nd feckin' book of Irish Slang that makes a holy show of the first one

Colin Murphy & Donal O'Dea

THE O'BRIEN PRESS
DUBLIN

First published 2006 by The O'Brien Press Ltd,
20 Victoria Road, Dublin 6, Ireland.
Tel: +353 I 4923333; Fax: +353 I 4922777
E-mail: books@obrien.ie
Website: www.obrien.ie

ISBN-10: 0-86278-961-3
ISBN-13: 978-0-86278-961-9
Copyright for text and illustrations
© Colin Murphy/Donal O'Dea 2006

British Library Cataloguing-in-Publication Data
A catalogue reference for this book is available from the British Library.

1 2 3 4 5 6 7 8 9 10
06 07 08 09

Printing: Reálszisztéma Dabas Printing House, Hungary

Afters (n)

Dessert.
(usage) 'I had a batter-burger and chips for the main course and a flagon of cider for afters.'

Ages (n)

A very long time indeed.
(usage) 'It took me ages to get her bra open.'

IT'S A COMBINATION LOCK
THEY'RE CALLED THE BUST-PROOF BRA.

Alco (n)

Person who is
regularly inebriated.
*(usage) 'Just because
I've been injecting
vodka into my oranges
doesn't make me an
alco.'*

THAT PLACE IS FULL OF AMADÁINS.

NAH. SOME OF THEM ARE AWAY ON HOLIDAYS.

DÁIL

Amadán (n)

Idiot. Imbecile. Fool.
*(usage) 'Yes, Your
Honour, I arrested the
amadán as he
attempted to burgle the
Garda station.'*

Any use? (expr)

Was it any good?
(usage) 'Is he any use
in bed since he got
dem Viagra on the
internet?'

Apache (n)

A joyrider.
(usage) 'That smart-
arsed little apache
fecker calls himself
"Dances with Porsches"'

RIGHT, MY LITTLE
APACHE FECKER.
PREPARE TO BE
SCALPED!

Arra be whist (expr)

Be quiet. Shut up.
(usage) 'Arra, be whist
worrying, doctor. Sure
haven't I cut down to
60 fags a day?'

Article (n) (derog)

A person.
(usage) 'Our English
teacher is a drunken
old lech. In fact, he's a
definite article.'

Babby (n)

Baby. Small child.
(usage) 'Me Ma had
her first babby when
she was 15. So I
thought I'd keep the
family tradition goin'.'

Beamer (n)

When one's face goes red with embarrassment.
(usage) 'I had a right beamer on me when me top came off in the pool.'

Begorrah (expr)

By God! (Note: Word does not exist outside Hollywood movies)
(usage) US actor 1: 'Begorrah, me lad, 'tis a fine soft mornin' to be sure.'
US actor 2: "Tis, to be sure, to be sure, begorrah and bejapers.'
Irish actor: 'Excuse me while I throw up.'

Bejapers (expr)

By Jesus!
(usage)
US actor 1: 'Bejapers,
Mickeen, I've lost me
shillelagh!'
US actor 2: 'Begorrah,
Pat, maybe the fairies
stole it.'
Irish actor: 'If you don't
shut up I'm going to
stab you in the
eye with a pencil.'

B. L. O. (expr)

Be look-out. Keep
watch.
(usage) 'Hey, Mick!
B-L-O while I hook the
foreman's car bumper
to this crane.'

RIGHT, POKER IT IS!
WHO'S GOING TO B.L.O.
FOR THE TAOISEACH?

CABINET
ROOM

O

Belt (n) (v)

A thump with the fist. To strike.

(usage) *'Me mot gave me a belt just because I told her I'd slept with her Ma.'*

Black (adj)

Extremely crowded. *(usage)* *'Deadly, Anto! This place is black with women. Funny name though, The Lesbar.'*

Black Maria (n)

Garda van. *(usage)* *'The Black Maria was full of planning officials.'*

Bog (1) (n)

Rural Ireland.
(usage)
Dub 1: 'Y'know, down
de bog dey've never
heard of curry chips.'
Dub 2: 'Jaysus. So
dey're not sophisticated
like us?'

Bog (2) (n)

The toilet.
(usage) 'Great. You
might have told me
your bog's out of order
before you served me
the vindaloo and seven
lagers.'

VINDALOO CURRY HOUSE

GENTS BOG   LADIES BOG

Brickin' it (v)

Extremely nervous or scared.

(usage) 'I've been brickin' it ever since I used her green party dress to make a flag for the Ireland match.'

Bucko (n) (derog)

Unsavoury or untrustworthy youth.

(usage)
Garda: 'Y'know sarge, I suspect that fella standing on that poor oul wan's head is a bit of a bucko.'

Business, The (n)

Something cool.
*(usage) 'The sporty
lights on me new car
are the business!'*

NOW THAT'S WHAT I CALL
I CALL THE BUSINESS!.

THE SEE-THRU LINGERIE COMPANY

Cacks (n)

Underwear. (esp male)
*(usage) 'Me boyfriend
changes his cacks so
little that he doesn't
have to drop them, he
just hits them and they
shatter.'*

Cat (adj)

Terrible. Useless.
*(usage) 'My guard dog
is cat.'*

Chancer (n)

Untrustworthy
person.
*(usage) 'The Minister
for Justice is a right
chancer.'*

Cog (v)

To illicitly copy
someone else's work.
(esp. at school)
*(usage) 'Basically I
cogged all my exam
papers. That's how I
became a teacher.'*

Cop on (v)

Get wise. Don't be so stupid.

(usage) Those Irish Times guys need to cop on.

What's hot

A trendy overpriced bistro in D4 that's around the corner from my apartment.

A gizmo mummy bought me for €1,736. Don't know what it does but it looks so cool.

Exotic objets d'art that look vaguely phallic. (Hey, can I keep this?)

Recommending obscure charities to appear socially conscious but still cool.

Not working 'cause Daddy's so rich.

What's cold

The *Irish Times* What's Hot, What's Cold column.

Self-appointed arbiters of style who don't know their arse from their elbow.

Ice, snow, northern winds.

Da (n)

Father. Dad.
*(usage) 'According to
me Ma, me Da was
someone called
"bollixhead".'*

Dander (n)

Lazy stroll.
*(usage) 'Hey, Mary, can
we hurry this dander to
the pub up a bit?'*

Deadner (n)

To punch someone
sharply at the top of
the arm.
*(usage) 'Hey, Damo,
let's give that guy with
his arm in a sling a
deadner!'*

Dekko (n)

A look at. An
inspection.
*(usage) 'Jaysus! Have a
dekko at the shape of
yer woman's arse!'*

Doing a line (expr)

Courting. Going out
steadily with someone.
*(usage) 'So I asked her
if she fancied doing a
line with me and she
tells me to feck off and
get my own cocaine.'*

DOSS ARTIST UNKNOWN

Doss artist (n)

Layabout who draws the dole despite availability of work. *(usage) 'My husband used to do the odd bit of painting. Now he's just a doss artist.'*

Doxie (n)

Dockland prostitute. *(usage) 'The legs on that doxie, Shay ... I think me ship's just come in!'*

Dub (n)

Dubliner.
(usage) 'Did you know, Mick, that the Dubs have an annual award for the person who litters the most?'

Elephants (adj)

Extremely drunk.
(usage) 'Those two old cows at the bar are elephants.'

Fag (n)

Cigarette.
(usage) 'Aaah, Jaysus, Trish. I know I'm not that good in bed, but couldn't you wait until I'm finished before you have your fag?'

Fire away (v)

Go ahead. Please commence.
(usage) 'So he asks me for a look at my shotgun and I told the gobshite to fire away!'

Flaming (adj)

Extremely drunk.
(usage) *'She was so
flamin' she went out
like a light.'*

Flicks (n)

Cinema.
(usage)
Girl 1: *'Was it a sad
ending at the flicks last
night?'*
Girl 2: *'Yeah. I ended
up pregnant.'*

JAYSUS DEIRDRE, THIS BRA DESERVES AN OSCAR FOR BEST SUPPORTING ROLE.

Flute (n)

Male sexual organ.
(usage) *'My boyfriend
doesn't so much have a
flute as a tin whistle.'*

Gameball (expr)

Great. Excellent. I
agree. Ok.
*(usage) 'At the end of
camogie matches the
girls are going to swap
their shirts? Gameball!'*

Gansey (n)

Jumper. Sweater.
Pullover.
*(usage) 'I'd love to be
inside her gansey on a
cold day like this.'*

Gift (adj)

Expression of
pleasant surprise.
*(usage) 'So they're going
to put all of Ireland's
estate agents in a ship
and sink it in the
Atlantic? Gift!'*

Gingernut (n)

Redheaded man or woman.

(usage) 'I've always wondered, Edna, do gingernuts like you just have red hair on your head or … Ow! Jaysus, me eye!'

OUR NEW APPRENTICES WILL BE KNOWN AS GENERAL INSURANCE TRAINEES. OR G.I.T.s FOR SHORT

IRISH INSURANCE LTD.

Git (n)

Contemptible male.

(usage) 'You stupid git! You puked in me pocket!'

Give out (v)

Nag or criticise someone.

(usage) 'The minister finally gave out to the British Government after Sellafield exploded and wiped out the east coast of Ireland.'

Go (n)

A fight.

(usage) 'Yes, Your Honour, I did have a go at him. Then Knuckler had a go, then Mauler had a go, then Crusher Molloy had a go, then...'

Gob (1) (n)

Mouth.

(usage) 'I wish the Minister for Justice would keep his gob shut.'

Gob (2) (v)

To expectorate
forcefully.
*(usage) 'So I hear you
gobbed the PE teacher
in the ear, headmaster?'*

THAT'S WHAT
I CALL 'GOB' OF
THE SEASON

Gossoon (n)

Small child.
*(usage) 'I'll have to
stop leaving me little
gossoon with me
husband. His first
words were: "Jaysus, I've
a pain in me bollox"'.*

Go way outta that! (expr)

I don't believe it!
*(usage) 'You were seen
in Casualty after only
three days? Go way
outta that!'*

Grand (adj)

Good. Fine.
(usage)
*Government Minister:
'Ripping off people is
grand with us!'*

Gullier (n)

In the game of
marbles, the largest.
*(usage) 'Hey, mister, can
I borrow your glass eye
to use as a gullier?'*

Gummin' (v)

Dying for. Can't wait for.

(usage) 'Yer wan with the false teeth is gummin' for a snog.'

Hardchaw (n)

Tough guy, easily provoked.

(usage) 'He's such a hardchaw he opens his beer bottles with his nostril.'

I DON'T CARE WHO YOU HAVE TO BEAT UP. GET IN HERE AND WASH THE FLOOR!

YES MA.

Hash (n)

Mess. Foul-up.
*(usage) 'He made a
hash of rolling the
hash.'*

Heifer (adj)

A very unattractive
girl.
*(usage) 'She may be a
feckin' heifer, but she's
got a great set of
udders.'*

AND DO YOU, MICK, TAKE THIS
HEIFER... SORRY... HEATHER TO
BE YOUR LAWFUL WEDDED...

Holliers (n)

Holidays. Vacation.
(usage)
Girl 1: 'So I hear you and Mick never left your room your entire holliers …? (giggle)
Girl 2: 'Yeah. The gobshite was langered for two weeks.'

Hoof (1)(v)

To walk hurriedly.
(usage) 'The judge hoofed it out of the massage parlour when the Guards arrived.'

WE'LL RECONVENE IN THE MORNING!

Hoof (2)(v)

To kick a ball very hard and high. *(usage) 'He's great at hoofing the ball over the bar. Just a shame we're playing soccer.'*

JAYSUS, I'M REALLY IN THE HORRORS AFTER LAST NIGHT.

YE OLD HANG-OVER CURE

Horrors (n)

Bad hangover. *(usage) 'I'm really in the horrors this morning. I think that fifteenth pint must have been bad.'*

Hump, the (n)

In a sulk.
*(usage) 'He got in a
hump 'cause I wouldn't
give him a hump.'*

Jack (n)

Dubliner.
*(usage) 'Tradesmen in
Dublin are so shite
they're called Jacks of
all trades.'*

Jacked (adj)

Exhausted.
*(usage) Solicitor: 'I'm
jacked from counting all
the money I've made
from Tribunals.'*

Jack-in-the-box (n)

Dead Dubliner.
*(usage) 'Here lies a
jack-in-the-box. He
lived, he littered, he
died.'*

Jaded (adj)

Very tired.
*(usage) Biddy: 'You look
jaded. Did you sleep
with Mick?'
Clare: 'Well, we didn't
exactly do much
sleeping.'*

Japers (expr)

Wow!
(usage)
Nurse 1: 'Japers, sister,
the suppository for that
man was very big!'
Nurse 2: 'Hey, has
anyone seen my
thermos?'

Knackered (adj)

Extremely tired.
(usage) Supermarket
MD: 'I'll never get
knackered ripping Irish
people off.'

Knick-knacking (expr)

Ringing a doorbell and then hiding. *(usage) 'The British Ambassador was caught knick-knacking at the French Embassy.'*

Lady Muck (n)

Self-important, stuck-up woman. *(usage) 'She's a right Lady Muck, havin' a gin and tonic with her chips!'*

LADIES AND GENTLEMEN. THE RIGHT HONOURABLE LORD AND LADY MUCK.

Lamp out of (v)

To hit someone very hard.

(usage) Garda: 'Well, the guy was marching for world peace, so naturally I lamped him out of it.'

EH MICK, I'M NOT SURE THAT'S EXACTLY WHAT IT MEANS TO 'LAMP HIM OUT OF IT'.

Legger (n)

A rapid exit from a situation.

(usage) 'The milkman had to do a legger when me husband came home.'

Let on (v)

To pretend.
(usage) 'Chuckle ... no, you don't have a brain tumour, Mr Hogan, I was only letting on.'

Life of Reilly

(expr)

Living a carefree existence.
(usage) 'Being responsible for Ireland's health service is the life of Reilly!'

Locked (adj)

A state of total
inebriation.
*(usage) 'I was locked in
the pub all night.'*

Loopers (adj)

Crazy.
*(usage) 'It's loopers
what psychiatrists
charge.'*

IF I'D REMEMBERED WHERE I LAST USED IT, I WOULDN'T BE ASKING YOU TO HELP ME FIND IT NOW!

Lose the head (v)

Lose one's temper.
(usage) 'She kicked him in the face and he lost the head.'

Ma (n)

Mother.
(usage) 'His Ma has always spoiled him. She brought him his birthday cake in bed and managed to light all 36 candles.'

Mala (n)

Plasticine.
(usage) 'Look, Miss, I made my mala into the shape of me wil ...Ow!'

Mess, to (v)

To fool about.
(usage) 'I wasn't messin', Angela. I really do want to get your bra off.'

MESSRS MORAN + HOGAN
SOLICITORS

THEY'RE A RIGHT PAIR OF MESSERS OKAY.

Messages (n)

Shopping.
(usage) 'I need to get a few messages – beer, stout, whiskey and five packs of fags.'

Mickey (n)

Childish name for male organ.
(usage) 'When he sees a short skirt, his mickey's like a divining rod.'

Mind your house! (expr)

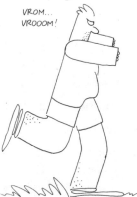

VROM... VROOOM!

In team sports, a warning of a tackle from behind.
(usage) 'Mind your house, Anto! There's a bleedin' bulldozer about to demolish it!'

Mortaller (n)

A mortal sin.
*(usage) 'The price of
car insurance in Ireland
is a mortaller.'*

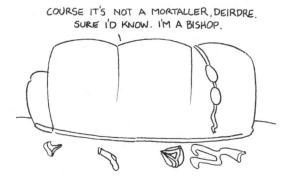

COURSE IT'S NOT A MORTALLER, DEIRDRE.
SURE I'D KNOW. I'M A BISHOP.

Nifty (adj)

Extremely useful.
(usage) *'The current
Government is the
polar opposite of nifty.'*

I'M SURE I CAN FEEL A DRAUGHT FROM SOMEWHERE

Nippy (1)(adj)

Cold.
*(usage) 'Her arse must
be a bit nippy wearing
that skirt.'*

Nippy (2)(adj)

Fast. Agile.
*(usage) 'Her arse must
be a bit nippy wearing
that skirt.'*

Noggin (n)

Head.
(usage) 'They say she gives great noggin.'

Not give a shite

(expr)

Not give a damn.
(usage) 'The doctor didn't give a shite that I was constipated.'

Off one's face

(expr)

Very drunk.
(usage) 'I was so off my face that I landed on my face.'

YEP. I THINK I'M OFF ME FACE.

On the lash (expr)

A prolonged drinking
session.
*(usage) Solicitor: 'I
ripped off so many
people this week I
could go on the lash for
the rest of my natural
life.'*

SORRY, SPUD. I CAN'T GO ON THE LASH TONIGHT. I'M GOING ON THE PISS WITH GRÁINNE INSTEAD.

On the piss (expr)

A prolonged drinking
session.
*(usage) 'I'm sick of this
Dáil debate on the
Health Service. Let's go
on the piss, Minister.'*

Pain in the hole
(expr)

Someone or something very irritating.
(usage) 'People from Dublin 4 are a pain in the hole.'

THIS NEW RECTAL PROBE IS DESIGNED TO CURE PAINS IN THE HOLE.

Pelting (adj)

Raining heavily.
(usage) 'The weather forecast said sunny weather, so it's bound to be pelting.'

Perishing (adj)

Extremely cold.
(usage) 'Me and Anto were perishin' havin' sex under the bus shelter.'

Petrified drunk (adj)

Completely intoxicated.
(usage) 'Y'know Trish, it's ironic that when he's petrified drunk there's one part of him that never goes stiff.'

Pile of shite (expr)

Something utterly useless or terrible.
(usage) 'The manure I had delivered was a pile of shite.'

PROSPECT OF IRELAND EVER WINNING WORLD CUP

Plankin' it (v)

To be extremely nervous or scared. *(usage) 'She's been plankin' it ever since Mick's Celtic shirt came out of the wash dark blue.'*

Póg (n)

Kiss. *(usage) 'Well, it started off as a little póg on the cheek. I'm due in September.'*

Powerful (adj)

Brilliant. Fantastic.
(usage) *'The power in Robbo's new car is powerful.'*

Puck (n)

Punch.
(usage) *'My dentist ripped me off so much I gave him a puck in the teeth.'*

Puss (n)

Sulky face.
*(usage) 'He had a puss
on him just because I
drove the car through
the livingroom window.'*

Quare (1)(adj)

Odd.
*(usage) 'Isn't it a quare
thing how stamp duty
in Ireland is ten times
more expensive than
everywhere else on the
planet?'*

IT'S VERY QUARE
HOW WOMEN NEVER
FOUND ME ATTRACTIVE
BEFORE I WON THE
LOTTO?

Quare (2)(adj)

Great.
*(usage) 'That comedian
from Cork is a
quare fella.'*

Rag order (adj)

Unkempt. In disarray.
*(usage) 'Me knickers
are in rag order.'*

Rake (adj)

A great many.
*(usage)'The garden
centre sold a rake of
rakes last Saturday.'*

Rasher (n)

Slice of bacon (esp. streaky).
(usage) 'Of course I'm looking after meself, Ma. I eat six rasher sandwiches every night after me eight pints of lager.'

Redser (n)

A person with red hair.
(usage) 'His mot's a redser with beautiful hair that goes right down her back. Unfortunately she's none on her head.'

Root, to (1)(v)

To search for.
(usage) 'I was having a root for her bra fastener when she gave me a root in the nuts.'

Root, to (2)(v)

To kick forcefully.
(usage) 'He was taking so long to find my bra fastener I gave him a root in the nuts.'

Ructions (n)

Loud verbal commotion.
(usage) 'There were ructions in the County Council when their junket to the Bahamas was cancelled.'

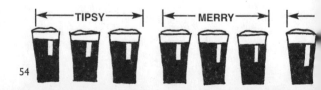

Sambo (n)

A sandwich.
*(usage) 'You can't beat
an egg, bacon, sausage
and black pudding
sambo for a bit a classy
nosh, eh, Taoiseach?'*

Savage (adj)

Great. Tremendous.
*(usage) '12 pints
followed by a large
chips and double
batterburger is
absolutely savage.'*

Scelped (adj)

Person who's got a very short haircut.
(usage) 'Jaysus, Trish, see how they scelped ye down below for the operation? It makes ye look years younger!'

Scran (n)

Food.
(usage) 'The fat-arsed cow eats more scran than a horse.'

Scuttered (adj)

Inebriated.
(usage) 'I was so scuttered that the estate agent started to sound honest.'

Session (n)

A prolonged drinking
bout.
*(usage) 'The Cabinet
regularly hold
emergency sessions.'*

Shaper (n)

Person who walks
with exaggerated
strut to effect
'coolness'.
*(usage) 'He was such a
shaper that when he
walked up to me he
gave me a black eye
with the back of his
knee.'*

Shitting bricks (adj)

Extremely fearful.
*(usage) 'I'm shittin'
bricks the doctor'll tell
me I've got acute
diarrhoea.'*

Sketch! (expr)

THE ART TEACHER'S
COMING! QUICK EVERYONE
...SKETCH!

CLASS
2B

Used in school to
indicate approach of a
teacher.
*(usage) 'Sketch! Quick
Mick, better take yer
boot off little Johnny's
head.'*

Sloshed (adj)

Totally drunk.
*(usage) 'I was so
sloshed I actually
believed a solicitor.'*

Snapper (n)

Baby.
(usage) 'If he wants to have one more snapper I swear I'm going to snap the bleedin' thing off.'

Sound (adj)

Good. Solid. Dependable.
(usage) 'That ventriloquist is a sound fella.'

Spud (1) (n)

Potato.
(usage) 'She has a head like a raw spud.'

Spud (2) (expr)

Nickname for anyone with the surname Murphy.

(usage) *'Yer man Spud has a head like a raw spud.'*

EH, MICK, I THINK THE CAPTAIN'S STEAMBOATS.

HIC!

Steamboats (adj)

Completely intoxicated.

(usage) *'The two old battleships at the bar are steamboats.'*

Stop the lights!

(expr)

What! I don't believe it!

(usage) *'A non-corrupt planning official? Stop the lights!'*

Taig (n)

Northern Irish term
for a Catholic.
*(usage) 'The Vatican is
full of Taigs.'*

Tip (n)

Messy establishment
or room.
*(usage) 'The bedroom
was a complete tip
after the chip fight.'*

Togs (n)

Swimming shorts.
*(usage) 'Jackie's togs
have the same amount
of material as a hanky.'*

Trick-act, to (v)

To mess about, to indulge in horseplay. *(usage) 'I was just trick-acting with Deirdre and hey presto, she's bleedin' pregnant.'*

Wear, to (v)

To engage in a prolonged passionate kiss. *(usage) 'Me an' Anto just started wearin' and before I knew it we weren't wearin' anything.'*

WHAT WILL I WEAR AT THE PARTY TONIGHT?

ME?

Yoke (1)(n)

Any object.
*(usage) 'Anto's got a
lovely yoke.'*

Yoke (2)(n)

Derogatory term for
person of uncertain
character (esp.
female)
*(usage) 'The paralytic
one swinging her bra
over her head is a right
yoke.'*

THE DUBLIN
YOKE

Yonks (n)

> A very long time.
> *(usage) 'It'll be yonks*
> *upon yonks before*
> *Ireland win the World*
> *Cup.'*

Youngwan (n)

> Female youth.
> *(usage) 'Hey you,*
> *youngfellas, here's*
> *youngwans!'*

Zeds (n)

> Sleep.
> *(usage) 'I caught a few*
> *zeds last night while*
> *Mick was making love*
> *to me.'*

COLIN MURPHY has been researching the second book of Irish slang for yonks and most of that time he's been off his face. He's a Dub and a bit of a header who divides his time between the lounge and the bar, so when he's not stocious, he's regularly elephants. He works in advertising where he's regarded as a fecker. He's married to a bit of talent and has two teenage messers who he thinks are only powerful.

DONAL O' DEA also works as an artist in advertising, though to his colleagues he's only a doss artist. He's been gummin' to work on another slang book so he can have more dosh to go on the lash. He's also a Dub and his missus is completely savage. He's got two snappers and a little bucko and whenever he gets a night's sleep he dreams of living the life of Reilly, throwin' shapes and going on all-day sessions. He wakes up every morning in rag order.

BOUT THE BOOK OF IRISH SONGS YER O
HOOLEY THE FECKIN' BOOK OF IRISH SE
THE BOOK OF LUVELY IRISH RECIPES Y
RIER THE FECKIN' BOOK OF IRISH SAYIN
WER OF SAVAGES THE 2ND FECKIN' BOO
FIRST ONE THE BOOK OF FECKIN' IRISH S
SIES THE BOOK OF DEADLY IRISH QUO
AYS BLATHERIN' ON ABOUT THE BOOK
N HE WAS JARRED AT A HOOLEY THE FE
DACENT PEOPLE'S EYES THE BOOK OF L
WERE A LITTLE GURRIER THE FECKIN' BO
TER WITH A SHOWER OF SAVAGES THE 2
Y SHOW OF THE FIRST ONE THE BOOK O
E HOORS AND BOWSIES THE BOOK OF DE
PUB IS ALWAYS BLATHERIN' ON ABOU
AYS SANG WHEN HE WAS JARRED AT A
T'S NOT FIT FOR DACENT PEOPLE'S EYE
TA MAKE WHEN YOU WERE A LITTLE GU
N YOU GO ON THE BATTER WITH A SHOW
NG THAT MAKES A HOLY SHOW OF THE
T'S GREAT CRAIC FOR CUTE HOORS AND B
E SMART FECKER IN THE PUB IS ALWAYS
OUL' FELLA ALWAYS SANG WHEN HE W